First Fire

A Cherokee Folktale

By Nancy Kelly Allen
Illustrated by Sherry Rogers

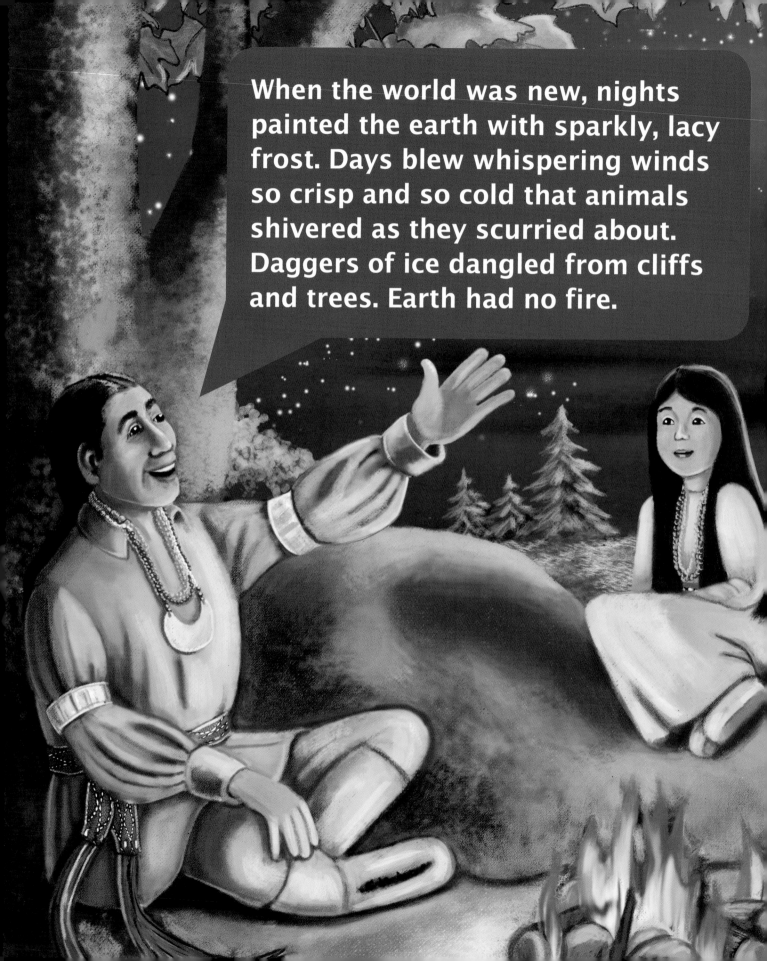

One day, the Thunders hurled a lightning bolt. A silver streak zigzagged out of the popping, cracking, cloud-patched sky. The bolt struck the bottom of a sycamore tree on an island. Flames sizzled.

The animals watched as puffs of smoke billowed out of the top of the tree.

They wanted the fire. They needed the fire. But a wide stretch of water surrounded the island.

A council of animals met and decided to bring back the fire. Every animal that could fly or swim wanted to be chosen to carry the fire across the water.

"I'm strong," said Raven. "I'll go."

The animals agreed. So Raven flew high, flew fast, flew far across the water and landed on the sycamore tree.

Raven perched on a branch and puzzled about how to carry back the fire. The heat scorched Raven's feathers black. Frightened, Raven returned to the animals without the fire. To this day, Raven's feathers are black.

"I'll get the fire," said Screech Owl. So Screech Owl flew high, flew fast, flew far across the water and landed on the sycamore tree.

A blast of fire flashed and burned Screech Owl's eyes. The owl finally found his way back to the animals, but without the fire. To this day, Screech Owl's eyes shine red in the bright light.

"Hoot Owl and I will fly together," Horned Owl said. So they flew high, flew fast, flew far across the water and landed on the sycamore tree.

An angry wind blew hot ashes that burned the feathers circling the owls' eyes. They returned without the fire. To this day, Hoot Owl and Horned Owl's eyes are circled with white rings.

"I'll get the fire," said Racer. The snake swam long, swam fast, swam far to the island and slithered into the smoky, fiery hole in the sycamore tree.

Heat scorched Racer's skin black. Racer twisted and turned to escape. The snake returned to the animals without the fire. To this day, Racer twists and turns in a slither and is as black as midnight.

The animals called another council meeting as snow painted the Earth white. They still had no fire. This time, each animal that could fly or swim had an excuse for why they could not bring home the fearsome fire.

At last, Spider said, "I'll go."

"How will you carry the ball of fire?" Raven asked.

"I have a plan," Spider answered as she ran long, ran fast, ran far on top of the water to the island. Along the way, she spun a thread from her body and wove it into a tusti—a bowl she carried on her back.

At the sycamore tree, Spider placed a tiny, hot coal into her tusti bowl and ran across the water back to the animals. To this day, Spider has her tusti bowl and the animals have fire.

For Creative Minds

Cherokee Then and Now

This story is a legend of the Cherokee people. Historically, the Cherokee lived in the mountains of southeastern North America. The Cherokee and their ancestors lived there for thousands of years! The Cherokee were once the largest nation of Native Americans.

Many stories have been passed down, from generation to generation. The storytellers made these tales come to life. They were dancers, actors, and singers. Some stories were a sacred part of the Cherokee religion. Other stories taught how to live or explained about the world.

The Cherokee culture is very much alive today! For modern Cherokees, like in most cultures, children learn the stories, history, religion, and language of their people from their parents, grandparents, and other adults. Storytelling is still an important part of the Cherokee culture. Cherokee children hear many of the same stories that other children listened to hundreds of years ago.

Cherokee Territory

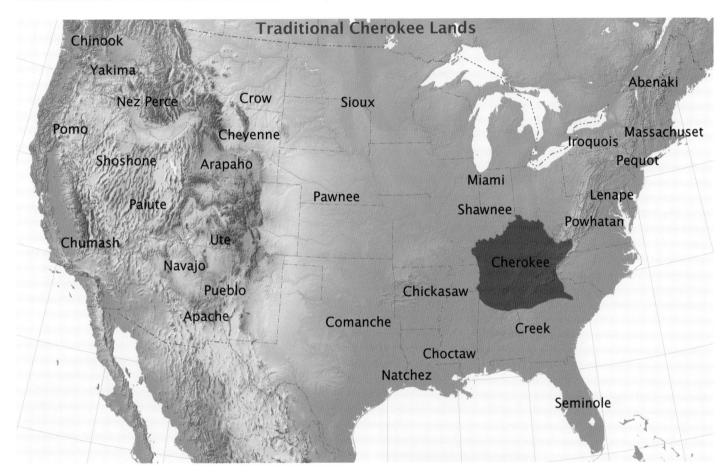

The map above shows the original lands of the Cherokee civilization. In the 1830s, the United States government forced the Cherokee out of their homes. The Cherokee were removed to Oklahoma. More than 4,000 died during this forced removal. This journey is called the Trail of Tears.

There are currently three Cherokee tribes recognized by the US government: the Cherokee Nation, Eastern Band of Cherokee Indians, and United Keetoowah Band of Cherokee Indians in Oklahoma. The Cherokee Nation is the largest of these three. The map to the right shows the **jurisdictional boundary** of the Cherokee Nation. "Jurisdictional boundary" means that this region is under the laws and government of the Cherokee Nation.

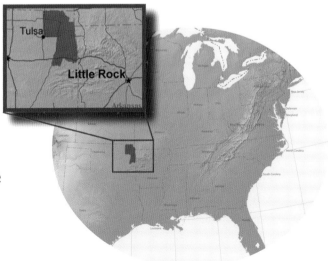

Cherokee Nation

Fire

Fire is very important for the entire natural world, including humans. Fire is a chemical reaction that uses fuel and oxygen to create heat and light.

Fire helps people stay warm when it is cold and be able to see when it is dark. Fire can cook food so that it is safe to eat. Small, controlled fires are useful, but if a fire gets too big or is out of control, it can be very dangerous.

Natural fires are usually started by lightning. Wildfires burn in forests and clear out old, dry wood. This helps return nutrients to the soil so that new plants can grow. These fires are normal and natural. The fires often die off on their own. If the weather has been very dry and hot, the fire can grow very large and threaten humans and animals.

True or False

1.   Fire is a physical reaction.
2.   Fire makes heat and light.
3.   Wildfires return nutrients to the soil.
4.   Fire can burn without any air.
5.   Fire is safe to play with.
6.   Forest fires are bad and should be put out immediately.
7.   Fire can make some foods safe to eat.
8.   Fire needs fuel to burn.
9.   All fires start because of humans.
10.   Fires won't start when it is cold.

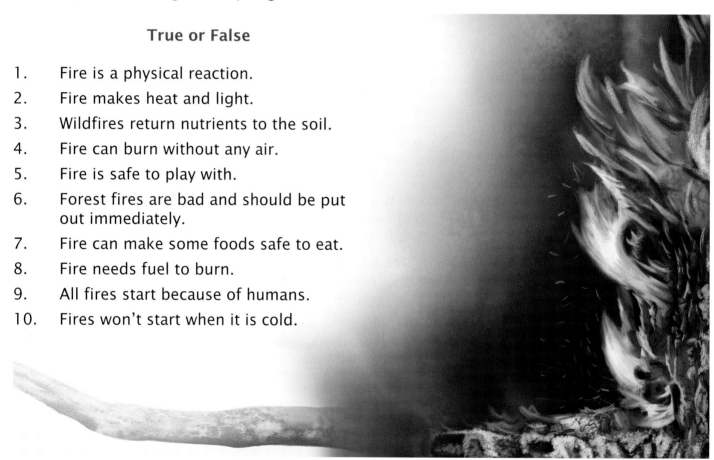

Answers: 1—False. It is a chemical reaction. 2—True. 3—True. 4—False. Fire needs oxygen to burn. 5—False. Fire can cause very painful burns. Always have a responsible adult with you when there is fire around. 6—False. Forest fires are necessary to clear out old plant matter. Small, naturally-occurring fires every few years can actually help to prevent major fires that threaten humans and animals. 7—True. Most raw meat and some raw plants can be dangerous to humans. Fire heats these foods until they are safe to eat. 8—True. Fire can use lots of different types of fuel, such as wood, coal, paper, and charcoal. 9—False. Lightning, lava from volcanoes, or sparks from falling rocks can start fires. 10—False. If there is good fuel and oxygen, fires can start even in cold weather. A nice, contained fire on a cold night can be just the thing you need to stay warm and cozy!

Water Spiders

"Water spider" is a common name for a spider that walks on or swims in the water. There are many different species of spiders that can do this. Some spiders, like the one in this story, spin webs that are used to hold or carry things. Match the description to the image.

wolf spider

water strider

1. Although they breathe air, these spiders live underwater. They trap air bubbles in the fine hairs on their stomach (abdomen) and legs. The female builds a bell-shaped web underwater that she fills with air. This bell provides a place for her to rest, mate, and raise her offspring. Newborn spiders are called **spiderlings**.

2. Spiders in this family live on every continent except Antarctica. Fine hairs on their legs allow them to spread out their weight so they can run across the water's surface. Instead of spinning webs to trap their prey, they chase them down! The females carry their eggs in ball-shaped **egg sacs** that they spin out of silk. After the spiderlings are born, their mother carries them on her back for a few weeks until they can survive on their own.

3. The females in this group of spiders are nearly twice as large as the males. They can grow up to 1 inch (2.6cm) long with a 3 inch (7.6cm) leg span. These spiders race out across the water to hunt. They usually eat aquatic insects, but some of the larger spiders can catch and eat small fish.

4. This insect is often called a "water spider," but is *not* a spider at all. Spiders have eight legs, but insects have only six. Even though they have wings, these insects cannot fly. Instead, they walk on the surface of the water.

fishing spider

diving bell spider

Answers: 1-diving bell spider. 2-wolf spider. 3-fishing spider. 4-water strider.

To the students at G.S. School . . . great readers, great writers, great people.—NKA

I would love to dedicate this book to my Cherokee Great Grandma Na Ni.—SR

Thanks to Gina K. Burnett, Outreach Coordinator at the Cherokee Heritage Center, for reviewing the accuracy of the information in this book.

Photo Credits

Image:	Photographer:
Diving bell spider	D. Kucharski K. Kucharska, Shutterstock
Fishing spider	Mark A. Musselman, U.S. Fish and Wildlife Service, Public Domain
Water Strider	Tim Vickers, Public Domain
Wolf Spider	McCarthy's PhotoWorks, Shutterstock

Library of Congress Cataloging-in-Publication Data

Allen, Nancy Kelly, 1949-
  First fire : a Cherokee folktale / by Nancy Kelly Allen ; illustrated by Sherry Rogers.
    pages cm
  ISBN 978-1-62855-207-2 (english hardcover) -- ISBN 978-1-62855-216-4 (english pbk.) -- ISBN 978-1-62855-234-8 (english ebook downloadable) -- ISBN 978-1-62855-252-2 (english ebook dual language enhanced) 1. Cherokee Indians--Folklore. 2. Fire--Folklore. I. Rogers, Sherry illustrator. II. Title.
  E99.C5A765 2014
  398.2089'97557--dc23

2013036735

Also available in Spanish as *El primer fuego: Una leyenda Chéroqui* and these other formats:
Spanish paperback ISBN: 9781628552256
English PDF ISBN: 9781628552348
Spanish PDF ISBN: 9781628552430
English ePub3 ISBN: 9781643510941
Spanish ePub3 ISBN: 9781643512525
English read aloud interactive ISBN: 9781628552522
Spanish read aloud interactive ISBN: 9781628552614

Lexile® Level: 730L
key phrases for educators:
fables/folktales, culture,
adaptations, anthropomorphic

Printed in China, November 2019
This product conforms to CPSIA 2008
Fourth Printing

Arbordale Publishing
formerly Sylvan Dell Publishing
Mt. Pleasant, SC 29464
www.ArbordalePublishing.com